Penguin
Rosh Hashanah

by Jennifer Tzivia MacLeod

Penguin Rosh Hashanah © 5774 Jennifer Tzivia MacLeod

ISBN-13: 978-1497573383
ISBN-10: 1497573386

It's difficult for a penguin
to get ready for Rosh Hashanah.

For one thing, he might
not have the right suit.

It's very cold in Antarctica, too.

There are no bees, no honey.
Just snow and penguins
for miles around.

Apples would be good,
but there are no trees
in Antarctica either.

No apples.

It's difficult for a penguin
to apologize to his
friends and family.

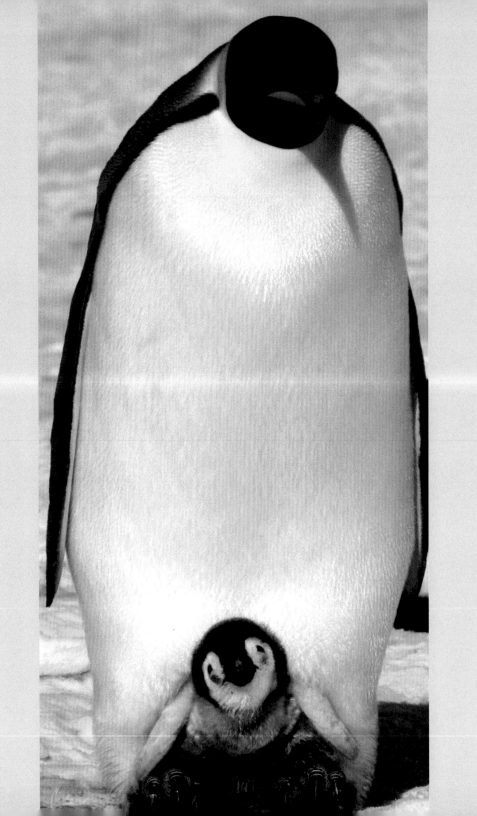

He can't help stepping on a few toes.

Sometimes, he's shy.
Sometimes, he's noisy.
He doesn't always listen
to his parents and teachers.

He doesn't always get along with friends.

But he sometimes forgets
why he's angry.
They forget too.

His parents help him all the time.

He doesn't always tell them
how much he loves them.

Everybody thinks penguins
are all alike.

Luckily, Hashem can tell
the difference.

It's difficult for a penguin
to get ready for a whole New Year…

But it's a nice feeling when
he's ready at last.

And it doesn't really
matter what suit he wears…

...It's just good to be
with friends and family.

Shanah Tovah!
שָׁנָה טוֹבָה!

Bonus:

How to fold your very own Origami Penguins:

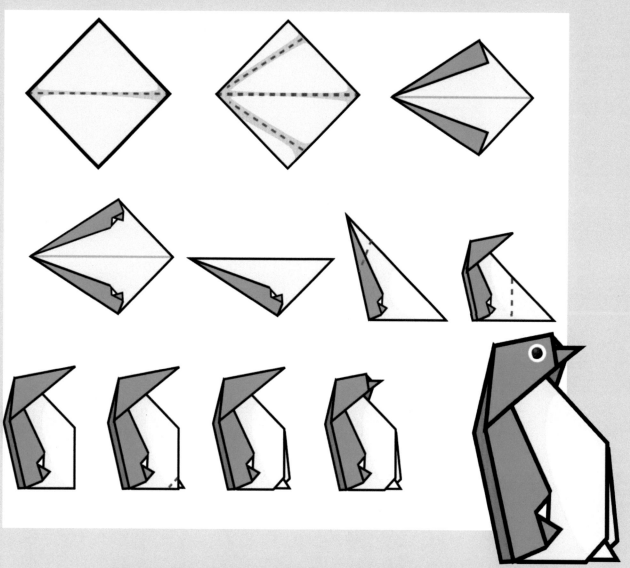

Hint: Use blue and silver or blue and white paper
to give your penguins a festive Rosh Hashanah look!

The Jewish Nature Series:

Penguin Rosh Hashanah

Animal Tashlich

Caterpillar Yom Kippur

Turtle Sukkot

Owl Hanukkah

Panda Purim

Otter Passover

Elephant Tisha b'Av

Come discover them all at
http://tinyurl.com/JewishNature

About the Author:

Jennifer Tzivia MacLeod is a proud mother of four (two big and two little), who recently moved to northern Israel. A freelance writer for magazines and newspapers, she also loves writing stories for her kids and their friends.

Can you help me out?

As an independent children's writer, I count on readers like you who leave feedback for others about my books. If you and your kids liked this story, please take a minute to leave a review:

http://tinyurl.com/PenguinRosh

Thanks! ☺

54737670R00018

Made in the USA
San Bernardino,
CA